For Ana

Love to Monika and Luka

Special Thank you to Claire Cartey

Drawings by Monika Melling

Two by Two and a half
by David Melling

First published in 2007
by Hodder Children's Books

Text and illustration copyright © David Melling 2007

Hodder Children's Books
338 Euston Road
London NW1 3BH

Hodder Children's Books Australia
Level 17/207 Kent Street
Sydney, NSW 2000

A catalogue record of this book is available from the British Library.

ISBN-13: 9780340903100
10 9 8 7 6 5 4 3 2 1

Colour Reproduction by Dot Gradations Ltd, UK
Printed in China

Hodder Children's Books is a division of Hachette Children's Books.

DAVID MELLING

Two by Two
and a half

h
Hodder
Children's
Books

A division of Hachette Children's Books

'Gather round everyone,'
cooed Miss Moo Hoo.

'Today we're going for a walk in the woods.

So pick a partner and tug my tail!'

Everyone found a partner except Little Bat Jack.

'I don't mind,' he said bravely – which was

just as well because the others

were already leaving.

As they went they

sang together:

'Follow the leader, follow the path,
two by two and a half.'

They hadn't gone far when
Rabbit heard a rustle
and a bustle.
It seemed to be coming from
the branches of a tall oak tree.
'What can it be?' she asked.
Everybody listened and
everybody trembled.

Miss Moo Hoo cupped
her ears and said,
'Is it the rumbling
tummy of…

...a tree-climbing
lion?'

'No! It's only Little Bat Jack,'
they sighed, 'and he doesn't count!'

'Follow the leader,
follow the path,
two by two and a half.'

Soon enough Duck felt and smelt a puff of warm wind,
and a musty, dusty cloud twirled around his feet.
'What can it be?' he asked.
Everybody felt it and everybody trembled.
Miss Moo Hoo pinched her nose and said,
'Is it the hot smoky breath of…

…a troublesome
dragon?'

'No! It's only Little Bat Jack,'
they sighed, 'and he doesn't count!'

'Follow the leader,
follow the path,
two by two and a half.'

This time it was Sheep who noticed something.
Up ahead she could see a wobbling wall of shadow!
'What can it be?' she asked.

Everybody looked and everybody trembled.
Miss Moo Hoo covered her eyes and said,
'Is it a naughty band of…

…rampaging

ragamuffins?'

'No! It's only Little Bat Jack,'
they sighed, 'and he doesn't count!'

'Time for lunch!'
panted Miss Moo Hoo.

But Wolf's tail began to bristle.

He heard a rustle and a bustle.

He felt a puff of warm wind.

He saw a wobbly wall of shadow.

'What can it be?' he gulped.

'Is it a snarling, prancing, growling, prowling bear?'

said Miss Moo Hoo.

'Run for the hills!'
bellowed Miss Moo Hoo.
But a bustly, snarly something
was blocking the way.
'Uh oh,' gulped the bear.

'HOORAY!'

they all cried.

'It's Little Bat Jack,

and HE DOES COUNT!'

Miss Moo Hoo, Rabbit, Sheep, Duck,
Wolf and Little Bat Jack all sat down
to eat their sandwiches.
Then they set off for home
singing as they went:

'Follow the leader,
front to back,
two by two AND
Little Bat Jack!'